Wol joins the family for dinner

All of a sudden there was a great *swooooosh* of wings—and there, on the windowsill, sat Wol. And he hadn't come empty-handed. Clutched in his talons was an enormous skunk. The skunk was dead, but he had managed to soak himself and Wol with his own special brand of perfume.

"Hoo-hoohoohoo-HOO!" Wol said proudly.

Which probably meant: "Mind if I join you? I've brought my supper with me."

Nobody stopped to answer. We three people were already stampeding through the door of the dining room, coughing and choking. Wol had to eat his dinner by himself.

Bantam Books by Farley Mowat
Ask your bookseller for the books you have missed

THE BOAT WHO WOULDN'T FLOAT
THE DOG WHO WOULDN'T BE
NEVER CRY WOLF
OWLS IN THE FAMILY
A WHALE FOR THE KILLING

OWLS IN THE FAMILY

Farley Mowat

Illustrated by Robert Frankenberg

A BANTAM SKYLARK BOOK

For Sandy and David
who had an owl
in their family too

*This low-priced Bantam Book
has been completely reset in a type face
designed for easy reading, and was printed
from new plates. It contains the complete
text of the original hard-cover edition.*
NOT ONE WORD HAS BEEN OMITTED.

RL4, IL4+

OWLS IN THE FAMILY
*A Bantam Book / published by arrangement with
Little, Brown & Company*

PRINTING HISTORY
*Little, Brown edition published March 1962
17 printings through October 1979
A Selection of Weekly Readers Children Book Club June 1969
A Junior Literary Guild Selection May 1952
Bantam edition / April 1981*

Illustrated by Robert Frankenberg.

ISBN 0-553-15094-4

Published simultaneously in the United States and Canada

PRINTED IN THE UNITED STATES OF AMERICA

0 9 8 7 6 5 4 3 2 1

Chapter 1

One May morning, my friend Bruce and I went for a hike on the prairie.

Spring was late that year in Saskatoon, Saskatchewan. Snowdrifts still clung along the steep banks of the river, in the shelter of the cottonwood trees. The river was icy with thaw water and, as we crossed over the Railroad Bridge, we could feel a cold breath rising from it. But we felt another breath, a gentle one, blowing across the distant wheat fields and smelling like warm sun shining on soft mud. It was the spring wind, and the smell of it made us walk faster. We were in a hurry to get out of the city and into the real prairie, where you can climb a fence post and see for about a million miles—that's how flat the prairie is.

The great thing about Saskatoon was the way it ended sharp all around its edge. There were no outskirts to Saskatoon. When you stepped off the end of the Railroad Bridge you stepped right onto the prairie and there you were—free as the gophers.

Gophers were the commonest thing on the prairie. The little mounds of yellow dirt around their burrows were so thick, sometimes, it looked as if the fields had yellow measles.

But this day Bruce and I weren't interested in gophers. We were looking for an owl's nest. We had decided that we wanted some pet owls, and if you want pet owls you have to find a nest and get the young ones out of it.

We headed for the nearest of the clumps of cottonwood trees that dot the prairies, and which are called "bluffs" out in Saskatchewan. The ground was spongy under our sneakers, and it squooshed when we hit a wet place. A big jack rabbit bounced up right under my feet, and scared me so much I jumped almost as high as he did. And as we came nearer the bluff, two crows came zooming out of it and swooped down on us, cawing their heads off.

Bluffs are funny places in the spring. The cottonwood trees shed a kind of white fluffy stuff that looks like snow. Sometimes it's so thick it comes right over the top of your sneakers and you get a queer feeling that you really *are* walking through snow, even though the sun on your back is making you sweat right through your shirt.

We walked through this bluff, scuffing our feet in the cottonwood snow and stirring it up in clouds. We kept looking up; and after a while, sure enough, we saw a big mess of twigs high up in a poplar.

"All right," Bruce said to the two crows which were swooping and hollering at us. "If you want me to snitch your eggs—I will!"

With that he handed me his haversack and began to shinny up the tree.

It was an easy climb, because cottonwood poplars always have lots of branches. When he got to the nest and looked into it I yelled up at him: "Any eggs?" Bruce grinned but he wouldn't answer. I could see him doing something with his free hand— the one he wasn't holding on with—and I knew there

were eggs there all right. I watched, and sure enough he was popping them into his mouth so he could carry them down out of the tree.

We always carried eggs down out of trees that way. The only thing was, crows' eggs are pretty big, and if you have to stuff three or four of them into your mouth it nearly chokes you.

Bruce started to climb down. When he got about ten feet from the ground he stepped on a rotten branch. Poplar branches are always rotten near the ground, and you have to watch out for them. I guess Bruce forgot. Anyway, the branch broke and he slid the rest of the way and lit on his seat with a good hard bump.

All the eggs had broken, and Bruce was spitting out shells and eggs all over the cottonwood snow. I got laughing so hard I couldn't even talk. When Bruce got most of the eggs spat out he came for me and tackled me, and we had a fight. It didn't last long, because it was too hot to really fight, so Bruce ate a sardine sandwich to get the taste of crows' eggs out of his mouth and then we started across the prairie again to search through other bluffs until we found an owl's nest.

I guess we searched about a hundred bluffs that morning, but we never saw an owl. We were getting hungry by then, so we made a sort of nest for ourselves on the ground, out of poplar snow and branches. We curled up in it and opened our haversacks.

Bruce had sandwiches and a lemon in his. He was the only boy I ever knew who liked to eat lemons. He said they were better than oranges, any day of the week.

I had a hard-boiled egg and just for fun I reached over and cracked the shell on Bruce's head. He yelled, and we had another fight, and rolled all over his sardine sandwiches.

We were just finishing our lunch when a wood gopher came snuffling along through the cottonwood snow. Wood gophers are gray and have big bushy tails. This one came right up to us and, when I held a crust out to him, he shuffled up and took it out of my hand.

"Got no sense," said Bruce. "You might have been a coyote, and then where'd he be at?"

"Heck," I said. "He's got more sense than you. Do I look like a coyote?"

The gopher didn't say anything. He just took the crust and scuttled away to his hole somewhere. We picked up our haversacks. The sun was as bright as fireworks and the sky was so clear you could look right through it—like looking through a blue window. We started to walk.

All of a sudden Bruce stopped so fast that I bumped into him.

"Lookee!" he said, and pointed to a bluff about half a mile away. There must have been a million crows around it. It looked as if the bluff was on fire and filling the sky with black smoke—that's how many crows there were.

When you see a bunch of crows all yelling their heads off at something, you can almost bet it's an owl they're after. Crows and owls hate each other, and when a crow spots an owl, he'll call every other crow for miles and they all join in and mob the owl.

We headed for that bluff at a run. The crows saw us coming but they were too excited to pay much attention. We were nearly deaf with their racket by the time we reached the edge of the trees. I was ahead of Bruce when I saw something big and slow go drifting out of one poplar into another. It was a great horned owl, the biggest kind of owl there is, and as soon as it flew, the whole lot of crows came swooping down on it, cawing like fury. I noticed they were careful not to get too close.

Bruce and I started to hunt for the nest. After a while, the owl got more worried about us than about

the crows and away he went. He flew low over the fields, almost touching the ground. That way the crows couldn't dive on him. If they tried it they would shoot past him and crash into the dirt.

There wasn't any owl's nest in that bluff after all, but we didn't worry. We knew the nest would have to be in some bluff not too far away. All we had to do was look.

We looked in different bluffs all afternoon. We found seven crows' nests, a red-tailed hawk's nest, and three magpies' nests. I tore the seat out of my trousers climbing to the hawk's-nest, and we both got Russian thistles in our sneakers, so we had sore feet. It got hotter and hotter, and we were so thirsty I could have eaten a lemon myself, except that Bruce didn't have any more.

It was past suppertime when we started back toward the railroad. By then we were pretending we were a couple of Arabs lost in the desert. Our camels had died of thirst, and we were going to die too unless we found some water pretty soon.

"Listen," Bruce said. "There's an old well at

Haultain Corner. If we cut over past Barney's Slough to the section road, we can get a drink."

"Too late," I told him. "Good-by old pal, old Sheik. I am doomed. Go on and leave me lay."

"Oh, nuts," said Bruce. "I'm thirsty. C'mon, let's go."

So we cut past Barney's Slough and there were about a thousand mallard ducks on it. They all jumped into the air as we went by and their wings made a sound like a freight train going over a bridge.

"Wish I had my dad's gun!" said Bruce.

But I was wondering why on the prairies they call lakes and ponds "sloughs." I still don't know why. But that's what they're called in Saskatoon.

There was one big bluff between us and Haultain Corner. It was too far to go around it, so we walked right through it. Anyway, it was cooler in among the trees. When we were about halfway through I spotted a crow's-nest in a big old cottonwood.

"Bet it's empty," I said to Bruce. But the truth was that I was just too hot and tired to climb any more trees. Bruce felt the same way, and we walked past. But I took one last look up at it, and there, sticking over the edge of the nest, was the biggest bunch of tail feathers you ever saw. My heart jumped right into my throat and I grabbed Bruce by the shirt and pointed up.

It was a great horned owl all right. We kept as quiet as we could, so as not to scare her, and then we looked around the bottom of the tree. There were bits of rabbits and gophers, and lots of owl pellets.

When owls catch something, they eat the whole thing—bones and fur and all. Then, after a while, they burp and spit out a ball of hair and bones. That's an owl pellet.

"By Gang! We found it!" Bruce whispered.

"*I* found it," I said.

"Okay," said Bruce. "*You* found it, then. So how about you climbing up and seeing how many young ones are in it?"

"Nothing doing, old pal," I replied. "*I* found the nest. So if *you* want one of the owlets, *you* climb up and have a look."

Neither of us was keen to climb that tree. The old owl was sticking close to her nest, and you can't always tell how fierce an owl is going to be. They can be pretty fierce sometimes.

"Say," said Bruce after a while, "why don't we just leave her be for now? Might scare her into leaving the nest for good if *we* climbed up. What say we get Mr. Miller, and come back tomorrow?"

Mr. Miller was one of our teachers. Bruce and I liked him because he liked the prairie too. He was a great one for taking pictures of birds and things. We knew he would be crazy to get some pictures of the owl—and Mr. Miller never minded climbing trees.

"Sure," I said. "Good idea."

We went off to Haultain Corner and got a drink of water that tasted like old nails, out of the broken pump. Then we walked on home. That night I told Dad about the owl's-nest, and he looked at Mother, and all he said was:

"Oh NO! Not owls too."

Chapter 2

The reason Dad said: "Oh NO! Not owls too" was because I already had some pets.

There was a summerhouse in our back yard and we kept about thirty gophers in it. They belonged to Bruce and me, and to another boy called Murray. We caught them out on the prairie, using snares made of heavy twine.

The way you do it is like this: You walk along until you spot a gopher sitting up beside his hole. Gophers sit straight up, reaching their noses as high as they can, so they can see farther. When you begin to get too close they flick their tails, give a little jump, and whisk down their holes. As soon as they do that, you take a piece of twine that has a noose tied in one end, and you spread the noose over the hole. Then you lie down in the grass holding the other end of the twine in your hand. You can hear the gopher all the while, whistling away to himself somewhere underground. He can hear you, too, and he's wondering what you're up to.

After a while he gets so curious he can't stand it. Out pops his head, and you give a yank on the twine. You have to haul in fast, because if the twine gets loose he'll slip his head out of the noose and zip back down his hole.

We had rats too. Murray's dad was a professor at the university and he got us some white rats from the medical school. We kept them in our garage, which made my Dad a little peeved, because he couldn't put the car in the garage for fear the rats would make nests inside the seats. Nobody ever knew how many rats we had because they have so many babies, and they have them so fast. We gave white rats away to all the kids in Saskatoon, but we always seemed to end up with as many as we had at first.

There were the rats and gophers, and then there was a big cardboard box full of garter snakes that we kept under the back porch, because my mother wouldn't let me keep them in the house. Then there were the pigeons. I usually had about ten of them, but they kept bringing their friends and relations for visits, so I never knew how many to expect when I went out to feed them in the mornings. There were some rabbits too, and then there was Mutt, my dog—but he wasn't a pet; he was one of the family.

Sunday morning my father said:

"Billy, I think you have enough pets. I don't think you'd better bring home any owls. In any case, the owls might eat your rats and rabbits and gophers. . . ."

He stopped talking and a queer look came into his face. Then he said:

"On second thought—maybe we *need* an owl around this place!"

So it was all right.

Sunday afternoon Bruce and I met Mr. Miller at his house. He was a big man with a bald head. He wore short pants and carried a great big haversack full of cameras and films. He was excited about the owl's-nest, all right, and he was in such a hurry to get to it that Bruce and I had to run most of the way, just to keep up with him.

When we reached the edge of the Owl Bluff Mr. Miller got out his biggest camera and, after he had fussed with it for about half an hour, he said he was ready.

"We'll walk Indian file, boys," he said, "and quiet as mice. Tiptoe . . . Mustn't scare the owl away."

Well, that sounded all right, only you can't walk quietly in a poplar bluff because of all the dead sticks underfoot. They crack and pop like firecrackers. Under Mr. Miller's feet they sounded like cannon shots. Anyway, when we got to the nest tree there was no sign of the owl.

"Are you sure this IS an owl's-nest?" Mr. Miller asked us.

"Yes, sir!" Bruce answered. "We seen the owl setting on it!"

Mr. Miller shuddered. "*Saw* the owl *sitting* on it, Bruce. . . . Hmmm. . . . Well—I suppose I'd better climb up and take a peek. But if you ask me, I think it's just an old crow's-nest."

He put down his big haversack and the camera, and up he went. He was wearing a big floppy hat to keep his head from getting sunburned and I don't think he could see out from under it very well.

"Boy, has he got knobby knees!" Bruce whispered to me. We both started to giggle and we were still giggling when Mr. Miller began to shout.

"Hoyee!" he yelled. "SCAT—WHOEEE! Hoy, HOY!"

Bruce and I ran around the other side of the tree so we could see up to the nest. Mr. Miller was hanging onto the tree with both arms and he was kicking out with his feet. It looked as if his feet had slipped off the branch and couldn't find a place to get hold of again. Just then there was a swooshing sound and the old owl came diving down right on top of him with her wings spread wide. She looked as big as a house and she didn't miss Mr. Miller by more than an inch. Then she swooped up and away again.

Mr. Miller was yelling some strange things, and good and loud too. He finally got one foot back on a branch but he was in such a hurry to get down that he picked too small a branch. It broke, and he slid about five feet before his belt caught on a stub. While he was trying to get loose, the owl came back for another try. This time she was so close that we could see her big yellow eyes, and both Bruce and I ducked. She had her claws stuck way out in front of her. Just as she dived toward him, Mr. Miller, who couldn't see her coming because of his hat, gave a jump upward to get free of the stub. The result was that the owl couldn't miss him even if she wanted to. There was an awful flapping and yelling and then away went the owl, with Mr. Miller's hat.

I don't think she really wanted that old hat. It was all Mr. Miller's fault for jumping at the wrong time. The owl seemed to be trying to shake the hat loose from her claws, but she couldn't, because her claws were hooked in it. The last we saw of her she was flying out over the prairie and she still had the hat.

14

When Mr. Miller got down out of the tree he went right to his haversack. He took out a bottle, opened it, and started to drink. His Adam's apple was going in and out like an accordion. After a while he put down the bottle and wiped his mouth. When he saw us staring at him he tried to smile.

"Cold tea," he explained. "Thirsty work—climbing trees in this hot weather."

"It was an owl's-nest, wasn't it, sir?" asked Bruce.

Mr. Miller looked at him hard for a moment. Then:

"Yes, Bruce," he said. "I guess it was."

There was one thing about Mr. Miller. You couldn't stop him for long. Now he explained to us that it was probably a bad thing to climb to the nest because it would disturb the owls too much. He had a better idea. He took a hatchet out of his haversack and we set to work building something that he called a "blind." What this was, really, was a little tent fixed on a platform of sticks high up in another tree, but close to the owl tree.

It took a couple of hours to build the blind. Bruce and I went scrounging for pieces of wood and, when we brought them back, Mr. Miller hauled them up the chosen tree with a rope and nailed them into place. When he had a platform built he hauled up the tent. The tent had a round hole, about as big as your fist, in the front of it. That was for the camera. According to Mr. Miller, you could hide in the blind and stay there until the owl thought everything was safe.

Then, when the owl came back to her nest, you could take all the pictures you wanted and she would never even know about it.

"He sure must think owls are dumb," Bruce muttered to me when Mr. Miller wasn't near. "She may not see him, but she could see that tent if her eyes were tight shut; and I don't think she's going to like it."

When the blind was finished, Mr. Miller said he was ready to try it.

"You boys go off for a walk," he told us. "Make a lot of noise when you're leaving. The books say birds can't count—so the owl will think all three of us have gone and she'll never guess I've stayed up here in the blind."

"Okay, Mr. Miller," I said. "C'mon Brucie, let's get going."

We walked about a mile away to a little slough and started looking for red-winged blackbirds' nests. It was another nice day and we forgot about Mr. Miller until we began to get hungry. Then we went back to the bluff.

Mr. Miller was on the ground. He had just finished the rest of his cold tea, but he didn't look the least bit well. His face was awfully white, and his hands were shaking as he tried to put his camera away. The camera looked as if it had fallen out of a tree. It was all scratched, and covered with dirt.

"Get some good pictures, sir?" I asked him cheerfully.

"No, I didn't," Mr. Miller said—and it was a sort of snarl. "But I'll tell you one thing. Any blame fool who says owls can't count is a liar!"

On the way home Mr. Miller finally told us what had happened.

About an hour after we went walking, the owl came back. She lit on her nest and then she turned around and took a good long look at the little tent, which was on a level with her, and only about six feet away.

Mr. Miller was busy inside the tent focusing his camera and getting ready to take the owl's picture, when she asked: "Who-WHO-OO-who-WHO-OO?"—and took one leap.

The next thing Mr. Miller knew the front was

ripped right out of the tent and the owl was looking him in the eye from about a foot away.

Mr. Miller accidentally dropped his camera; and then of course he had to hurry down to see if it was all right. And that was when we got back to the bluff.

I guess it wasn't a very good day for Mr. Miller, but it wasn't too bad for us. Mr. Miller said he had seen three young owls in the nest and he thought they were about halfway grown, which meant they were about the right age to take home for pets.

All we had to do now was to figure some way to get hold of them.

Chapter 3

The next week seemed awfully long. The only time I really hated school was during the springtime—particularly in May when the birds were busy nesting on the prairies. This May week, what with thinking about the owls, and sitting by the open window sniffing the smells of springtime, I wished school had never been invented.

Every recess, and after school, Murray and Bruce and I talked about the young owls and tried to think of ways to get them out of their nest. Murray suggested we should cut down the tree; but that was too dangerous because the young owls might be hurt. Bruce said he might get his father to come and shoot the old owl so it would be safe for us to climb the tree; but that wasn't fair.

The only thing I could think of was firecrackers. My idea was to get some small skyrockets and let them off under the nest to scare the mother owl away. The trouble was that we had no money and, anyway, the storekeepers wouldn't sell skyrockets to kids our age.

Then, on Friday night, we had a storm of the kind called a "chinook." Chinooks come down out of the Rocky Mountains in Alberta and sometimes they blow right across Saskatchewan—and they blow like fury. Lying in my bed on Friday night I could hear branches snapping off the poplar trees along the riverbank. The rain was pelting on the roof so hard that it scared Mutt (who always slept on my bed) and made him howl. I had to pull a quilt over his head to make him keep quiet. He hated storms. I worried about the young owls for a long time before I finally fell asleep.

Early on Saturday morning Murray called for me and we met Bruce at the Railroad Bridge. It was a fine morning and the sun kept popping in and out between the white clouds that were racing across the sky trying to catch up to the chinook. Everything was steaming from all the rain, and the prairie was soggy wet.

We hurried across the fields and didn't care if our feet did get soaked, because we were worried about the owls. When we were still quite a way from Owl Bluff, Bruce gave a shout:

"Lookee!" he yelled. "Old Miller's blind is gone!"

Sure enough, six or seven of the biggest cottonwoods were snapped right off at the tops and, as for Mr. Miller's blind, it had been blown clean out of its tree and nobody ever did find it again. But the worst thing was the owl's-nest. The rain and wind had smashed it to pieces, and all that was left was a stick or two stuck in the crotch where the nest had been.

There was no sign of the old owls at all; but on the ground near the foot of the tree were two young owls—and they were cold and dead. They were so young they had grown only about half their feathers, and baby-down was still sticking to them all over. I don't know whether they were killed by the fall, or not; but they were as wet as sponges and I think they probably died from being so wet and cold all night long.

We felt as miserable as could be, and all we could think of to do was to have a funeral for the little owls. Bruce had his jackknife with him and he started to dig a grave while Murray and I went looking for the right kind of sticks to use for crosses. There was a big pile of brush nearby, and I happened to give it a kick in passing. Something went *snap-snap-snap* from under it. I shoved my hand under the brush and touched a bundle of wet feathers.

Bruce and Murray came over and we pulled the brush away. There was the missing owlet, the third one that had been in the nest, and he was still alive.

He was bigger than the other two, and that was probably because he was the first one hatched. Horned owls are funny that way. They begin to lay their eggs in March when it's still winter on the prairie. The eggs are laid a few days apart, but from the time the first one is laid, the mother has to start "setting." If she waited until she had a full clutch of eggs, the early ones would be chilled and would never hatch. The first egg that's laid hatches first, and that young owl gets a four- or five-day head start on the next one who, in turn, gets a head start on the next one.

The one we found must have been the first to hatch because he not only was bigger than the others but must have been a lot stronger too. When the nest blew apart, and he fell to the ground, he was able to wiggle under the brush pile for shelter, and that probably saved his life.

He was about as big as a chicken, and you could see his grown-up feathers pushing through the baby down. He even had the beginnings of the two "horn" feathers growing on his head. A surprising thing about him was that he was almost pure white, with only small black markings on the ends of his feathers. When we found him he looked completely miserable, because all his down and feathers were stuck together in clumps, and he was shivering like a leaf.

I thought he would be too miserable to feel like fighting, but when I tried to pick him up he hunched forward, spread his wings, and hissed at me. It was a good try, but he was too weak to keep it up, and he fell right over on his face.

I was still a little bit afraid of him, because his claws were long and sharp, and his beak—which he kept snapping—seemed big enough to bite off my finger. But he did look so wet and sad that after a while I stopped being afraid. I got down on my knees in front of him and, very slowly, put my hand on his back. He hunched down as if he thought I was going to hurt him, but when I didn't hurt, he stopped hissing and lay still. He felt as cold as ice. I took off my shirt and put it over him, and then I picked him up as carefully as I could and carried him out of the bluff so he could sit in the sunshine and get dry and warm again.

It was surprising how fast he started to get better. In half an hour his feathers were dry and he was standing up and looking around him. Murray had brought along some roast-beef sandwiches for lunch. He took some meat out of the sandwiches and held it out to the owl. The owl looked at him a min-

ute, with its head on one side, then it gave a funny
little hop and came close enough to snatch the meat
out of Murray's fingers. It gave a couple of gulps,
blinked its eyes once, and the meat was gone.

He was certainly a hungry owl! He ate all the
meat we had, and most of the bread as well. When I
found some dead mice that his mother must have
left on the edge of the nest, and which had also been
blown to the ground, the owl ate them too. They
must have been hard to swallow, because he ate
them whole. But he got them down somehow.

After that we were friends. When Bruce and I
started to walk away from him, just to see what he
would do, the owl followed right along behind us

like a dog. He couldn't fly, of course; and he couldn't walk any too well either. He kind of jumped along, but he stayed right with us all the same. I think he knew he was an orphan, and that if he stayed with us we'd look after him.

When I sat down again, he came up beside me and, after taking a sideways look into my face, he hopped up on my leg. I was afraid his claws would go right through my skin, but they didn't hurt at all. He was being very careful.

"Guess he's your owl, all right," Bruce said, and I could see he was a little jealous.

"No, sir, Bruce," I replied. "He can live at my place, but he's going to be our owl—all three of us."

We left him sitting in the sun by the haversacks and then we buried the other two little owls and had a funeral over them. After that we were ready to go home.

We decided the best way to carry our new pet was to put him in my haversack. He didn't like it much, but after a struggle we managed to stuff him into it. We left his head sticking out so he could see where he was going.

Mutt and Bruce's dog, Rex, hadn't been with us that morning. I think the two of them had gone off cat-hunting before we got up. But as we were walking along the sidewalk in front of my house, we met old Mutt coming back from wherever he had been.

Mutt was cross-eyed and shortsighted, and so he never could see any too well. He came up to me to say hello, wagging his long tail and sniffing me—and then suddenly he smelled owl. I don't think he knew exactly what it was he smelled, because he had

never been close to an owl before. But he knew he smelled something strange. I stood there trying not to laugh while he sniffed all around me. He snuffed my trousers and then he began to sniff the haversack. When his nose was nearly in the owl's face, the bird opened its beak and snapped it shut again right on the end of poor old Mutt's black nose. Mutt gave a yelp you could have heard a mile away, and went loping off to hide his hurt feelings under the garage.

We put the owl in the summerhouse and when Dad got home from work the owl was sitting on the orange crate watching the gophers running around on the floor below him. It kept him busy. His head kept turning one way and then the other until it looked as if he were going to unscrew it right off his shoulders. He didn't know what to make of the gophers, because he had never seen a live one before. But he was certainly interested in them.

"Better count your gophers, Billy," said my father. "I have an idea they may start disappearing. By the way, what do you call your owl?"

I hadn't thought of any name for him up until that moment, but now one just popped into my head. I remembered Christopher Robin's owl in *Winnie-the-Pooh*.

"His name is Wol," I said.

And Wol he was, forever after.

Chapter 4

I woke up early on Sunday morning, while everyone else in the house was still asleep. I sneaked downstairs in my pajamas and went out into the back yard to see how Wol was getting along. The grass was still wet with dew, and it was cold and slippery under my bare feet.

I peeked through the screen of the summerhouse but for a while I couldn't see Wol. He had got down off his orange crate and was standing in the shadows, on the floor. There wasn't a single gopher in sight, and I had an awful moment as I wondered if he had eaten the lot of them. Then I realized this was silly, for there had been thirty gophers—and he was only one small owl.

Wol didn't see me. He seemed fascinated by a pile of old sacks lying in a corner and, as I watched, he made a hop and a skip and jumped up on top of the sacks.

Then we both found out where the gophers were. I never saw so many gophers move so fast. They came shooting out from under the sacks like bullets, and they went crazily bouncing from side to side of the summerhouse looking for some new place to hide.

I guessed what had happened. Wol must have been feeling lonely, and so he decided to make friends with the gophers. But if Wol didn't know anything about gophers, the gophers knew all about owls. When he plopped down among them they must have run for shelter under those sacks as if the devil himself was after them.

Now that Wol had accidentally (or was it on purpose?) chased them out into the open again, they went mad. One big fellow came zooming against the wall, bounced off it, and ran headlong into Wol. Wol jumped, fluffed his feathers, and gave a surprised little hoot. The gopher probably thought his last moment had come, but anyway he wasn't going to die like a coward; so he bit Wol on the leg.

Wol exploded. One minute he was on the floor, and the next he was clinging upside-down to the screening at the top of the summerhouse. He was scared to death. I don't think anything in the world could have persuaded him to go back down there among those bouncing, biting gophers.

I went into the summerhouse and untangled Wol from the screening and took him outside. He was so glad to see me that he started to hoot and couldn't stop. It was like hiccups. I couldn't put him back with the gophers, so I tucked him under my arm, tiptoed back into the house and upstairs to my room.

My bedroom was on the third floor, right up under the roof. Nobody ever came up there except me and the maid, whose name was Ophelia (we always called her Offy), who made my bed and tried to dust the room. I knew perfectly well Mother would never allow me to keep Wol in the house, but I was pretty sure that if I could just keep him locked in my room, and could hide him under the bed when Offy was due, nobody would know.

When I went downstairs for breakfast about an

hour later I left Wol sitting on the back of a chair acting quite at home. I *thought* I closed the bedroom door tight, but the latch must have slipped.

Dad and I had breakfast together, but Mother wasn't feeling well that day so she decided to have hers in bed. After Offy had brought me my porridge, she went into the kitchen and got a breakfast tray ready for Mother.

Offy was an odd sort of girl. She used to have queer dreams. She claimed she used to see angels and things in her dreams. Sometimes she saw them when she was supposed to be wide awake. But she was a good cook, and so Dad and Mother never bothered much about the things she claimed she saw.

Offy took the breakfast tray and started up the back stairs. These stairs were dark and spooky because there was no window opening on them. About halfway up the stairs she met Wol on his way down.

Offy gave a terrible yell and dropped the tray. Wol, who was still nervous after the trouble with the gophers, let out a hoot, and tried to fly. He and Offy arrived at the bottom of the stairs together, all in one flapping lump.

After my father got her quieted down, Offy went straight to her room and packed her bags. She marched out of the house without even saying good-by to Wol and me—and none of us ever saw her again.

Dad was unhappy.

After breakfast he called me into his study for a talk.

"Billy," he said, "if that owl ever comes into this

house again, he goes into the roasting pan; and as for you, you'll get a licking you'll remember for a week!"

But my father never stayed mad long. The very same afternoon he got out his carpenter's tools and he and I worked until suppertime making a special cage for Wol. It was a big cage, about ten feet square, and covered all over with chicken wire. It was built around the stump of a dead tree which stood in the back yard; and on the side of the tree Dad nailed a wooden box, as a place where Wol could go to keep dry if it rained.

Wol liked the new cage all right; the only trouble was that he got lonely when he was left in it. As long as Murray or Bruce or I was with him he was perfectly happy; but when there was nobody around he would sit on the tree stump all hunched-up, looking miserable. I tried putting some pigeons in to keep him company, but they were scared of him, and he was nervous of them, so that didn't work.

About two weeks later, the problem solved itself.

It was a Tuesday and I was biking home from school along the alley behind our block. As I came along I saw a couple of kids standing beside a big oil-drum and dropping stones into it. One of the kids was Georgie Barnes, but the other was a big kid I didn't know.

Georgie saw me coming and gave a yell: "Hi Billy! Come over here and have some fun!"

What those two kids were doing wasn't fun at all. In the bottom of the barrel was a baby owl and, for a minute, I thought it was Wol, until I saw it was smaller, and a lot darker in color. It was the dirtiest bird

I ever saw. Its feathers were all ruffled and broken, and it was smeared with oil. The kids were dropping stones on it, and every time a stone hit it, it would scrunch down and make a weepy noise, like a tin whistle with a tremble in it.

I wanted to tell them to stop dropping stones, but I knew that would mean a fight, and I knew I couldn't lick the two of them.

"Where'd you get it?" I asked the big kid.

"What's it to you, shorty?"

"Well," I said, "I have a kind of a zoo at my place and I could sure use an owl."

"Whatcha gimme for him?"

"Give you my Scout knife."

"Let's have a look."

I showed it to him and he opened all the blades and then he said: "It ain't much good. But this here owl ain't much good either. Pretty near dead. O.K. kid, it's yours."

Funny how some kids are. One minute Georgie Barnes was trying to kill the little owl with stones, but the moment I bought it he began to act as if he wanted to be its nurse. He climbed into the barrel and handed it out to me, and then he followed me home and helped me clean some of the oil off it with a rag. He told me the big kid had found an owl's-nest in a bluff near Sutherland, and had shot the old owl and all but one of the young ones with his .22 rifle. He only brought the last young one home as a sort of joke he was going to play on his dog.

It was a pretty sick little owl. I guess it hadn't eaten anything for a long time, and the stones and the oil hadn't done it any good either. It was too sick to sit on a branch of the tree in Wol's cage, so I put it on the floor of the cage while I went to the house to get some hamburger for it.

When I got back, the new owl was lying on its side and Wol was standing over it. I thought he must have taken a whack at it; but Georgie said No, that wasn't what had happened. Georgie said the new owl had just fallen over by itself, and when Georgie tried to pick it up again, Wol jumped down out of the tree and wouldn't let Georgie near it.

When I went into the cage and held some meat out toward the new owl, Wol hunched down, spread his wings and hissed at me as if he were saying: "You leave that bird alone, or you'll have me to deal with!"

"Easy, there!" I told him. "Take it easy, Wol. This little fellow's hungry, and I'm just going to feed him."

I don't know if Wol understood me, but he stopped hissing anyway. I held some bits of hamburger against the new owl's beak and after a while he took a piece. Finally he ate the whole lot, and then he staggered to his feet and stood there, swaying back and forth. Before I could touch him, Wol sidled over until the new owl was leaning right against him. Then the new bird closed his eyes and seemed to go to sleep.

That's the way we left them. By the next morning the new owl was up on the branch with Wol, and from that time on, Wol was never lonely.

When Dad got home from the office that eve-

ning, I told him all about it. I told him the new one was called Weeps, because of the weepy-whistle noise he made all the time.

"*Two* owls!" my father cried, and banged his hand against his forehead. "Now we'll never get another maid! All right, Billy. BUT NO MORE OWLS—you understand?"

He needn't have worried. Two owls was all I wanted, anyway.

Chapter 5

Though there were only a few more weeks left of school before the summer holidays began, each day seemed a hundred years long. I could hear the river boiling over the sand bars as I sat at my desk, and I could smell the sticky-sweet smell of the young poplar leaves. Our school stood right beside the river, and every now and then a flock of ducks would go over the playground, *quack-quack-quacking* as if they were laughing at us for being stuck inside, while they were flying free across the wide prairie. What made it even worse, for me, was just sitting there wondering what my owls were doing.

After school I would jump on my bike and pedal like forty over the bridge and down our street. When I got close to home I would give a couple of owl-whoops to let Wol and Weeps know I was coming. By the time I skidded into the yard and parked my bike, they would be tramping impatiently up and down the cage. As soon as the door was open they would come waddling out as fast as they could, ready for play.

Wol liked to scramble up on the back of an old lawn chair, then he would take a wild leap and try to land on my shoulder. If he missed, he would nose-dive into the lawn; but it never bothered him much. He would hop back to the chair, climb up, and try again until finally he made my shoulder.

Weeps was different. He never believed he could

do anything by himself, and so he would just sit on the lawn and whimper until I picked him up and put him on my other shoulder. I think Weeps's spirit must have been broken in the oil drum, because as long as I knew him he was always afraid of doing things.

With both owls riding on my shoulders I used to go down the street to where our gang played games in an empty lot. Can-the-can was a favorite game that spring; sort of a combination of baseball and football. We used an inflated rubber beach ball that belonged to Murray, and when all the kids got chasing it, Wol would get so excited he would join in too. One time he got in the way of the ball just when someone kicked it, and it knocked the wind clean out of him. The next time the ball came near him he made a jump and got hold of it with both sets of claws. There was a hissing noise and the ball went limp. Wol was pleased as punch, but *we* weren't, because it was the only ball we had.

All the kids, except Bruce and Murray, were a bit scared of the owls, so when I had them on my shoulders I could go anywhere in Saskatoon and be safe as houses. Even the tough kids down by the flour mill kept their distance when I had the owls with me. Those owls were better bodyguards than tigers.

Wol and Weeps grew fast. Weeps would eat anything he could get and still be hungry; but Wol was fussy about his food. At first Wol would only eat cooked butcher's meat, hard-boiled eggs and fig cookies. Later on he would eat anything that came from our table, even vegetables. (All except parsnips, which he hated.) Occasionally both owls would eat a dead gopher that some kid had shot or snared as a present for them; but they didn't really like their supper raw.

By the middle of June, when they were three months old, my new pets had reached full size. Wol was a little bigger than Weeps and stood about two feet high; but his wingspread was nearly five feet across! The claws of both were about an inch long and as sharp as needles ; and their big hooked beaks looked strong enough to open a tin can. Weeps was a normal owl color, sort of a mottled brown, but Wol stayed almost pure white, with just a few black markings on his feathers. At night he looked like a ghost.

Although they were grown-up now, neither of the owls seemed to know what his wings were for. Because they saw us walking around, they seemed to think they had to walk around too. Maybe if I had been able to fly, they would have learned to fly a lot sooner; but the way things were, both owls tried to do what we kids did. They saw us climbing trees, and so they took to climbing trees.

It was pretty silly to watch Wol climbing. He used to really climb. First he'd jump up to a low branch and then he'd use his beak and his claws to half-lift himself and half-shinny to the next branch. My pigeons used to circle around sometimes and watch him. They must have thought he was crazy. People sometimes thought so too. One day Wol was climbing a poplar in our front yard when a man and a woman stopped on the sidewalk and watched him, with their mouths open.

Finally the man said to me: "What on earth's the

matter with that bird? Why doesn't he *fly* to the top of the tree?"

"He can't fly, sir," I replied. "He never learned how."

The man looked at me as if I were crazy too, and walked off without another word.

The day Wol actually learned to fly was one I'll remember for a long time. He had climbed a cottonwood in the back yard and had got way out on a thin little branch, and couldn't get back. You never saw an owl look so unhappy. He kept teetering up and down on the end of the branch, and *Hoo-hoo-HOOING* at me to come and get him out of his fix.

Dad and Mother came out to see what was going on, and they started to laugh; because who ever heard of a bird that couldn't get itself down out of a tree? But when people laughed at Wol it hurt his feelings and upset him.

What with the laughter, and the fact that it was suppertime and he was hungry, Wol got careless. Finally he teetered a little too far forward and lost his balance.

"Hoo-HOOOOOO!" he shrieked as he bounced through the branches towards the ground. Then, all of a sudden, he spread his wings; and the next thing any of us knew, he was flying . . . well, sort of flying. Not having done it before, he didn't really know what he was doing, even then.

You could tell he was just as surprised as we were. He came swooshing out of the tree like a rocket, and he seemed to be heading straight for me; but I ducked and he pulled up and went shooting back into the air again. He was still *hoo-hooing* like mad when he stalled and slid back, downward, tail-first, and hit the ground with an awful thump.

By that time I was laughing so hard I had to lie on the grass and hold my stomach. When I looked up at last, it was to see Wol stomping into his cage. He was furious with all of us, and I couldn't persuade him to come out again until next day.

At supper that night my father said: "You know, I don't believe that owl realizes that he's an owl. I believe he thinks he's a human being. You'll have to educate him, Billy."

It wasn't quite as bad as that. Wol eventually did learn to fly pretty well, but he never seemed to like flying, or to trust it. He still preferred to walk wherever he was going.

Weeps never learned to fly at all. I tried to teach him how by throwing him off the garage roof, but he wouldn't try. He would just shut his eyes, give a hopeless kind of moan, and fall like a rock without even opening his wings. Weeps didn't believe he could fly, and that was that.

Just before school ended, Wol learned a new trick which bothered me a lot. He discovered that if he took a good swipe at it with his claws, he could tear a hole in the chicken wire of the cage. Once he learned to do this it was impossible to keep him penned up when he didn't want to be.

This worried me because there were a lot of tough alley cats, and tough dogs too, in Saskatoon. I was afraid if one of them ever got hold of Weeps or Wol, when I wasn't around, then that would be the end.

After a look at the owls' claws and beaks, Mother said she thought it would be the end of any cat or dog that tackled Wol or Weeps; but I still worried.

One night Wol had a little argument with Mutt about a bone, and Wol got mad and wouldn't come down out of his tree to go to his cage at dusk. I called him and called him, but he just ignored me, and finally I had to go off to bed and leave him out.

I slept pretty lightly that night, with one ear cocked for trouble, because I knew the cats would be about. Sure enough, just at dawn I heard a squawk and a scuffling noise outside. I hopped out of bed, grabbed my air gun, and whipped out of the house as fast as I could.

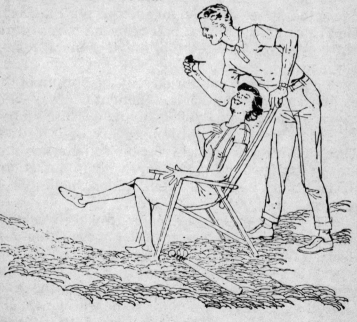

Wol wasn't in the tree. In fact there was no sign of him anywhere in the front yard. I raced around the corner to the back, expecting to find him dead and eaten; but, instead, I found him asleep on the back porch steps. He had his feathers ruffled out the way birds do when they are asleep, and it wasn't until I got right up to him that I saw the cat.

Wol was sitting on it, and only its head and tail stuck out beneath his feathers; but enough was showing so I could see that this cat wasn't going to bother anybody any more.

I pulled Wol off, and he grumbled a little bit. I think he'd found that cats made good foot-warmers.

It was a big ginger tomcat, that lived two doors down the street and belonged to a big man who didn't like kids. This cat had been the terror of the birds, other cats, and even of the dogs in our neighborhood, for years.

I got a shovel and buried it at the bottom of the garden. I suppose the cat had thought Wol was some new kind of chicken. Well, he found out differently.

Dogs were no problem to my owls either. Though Mutt was no owl-lover himself, he wouldn't let any strange dog chase them—not without a fight. Several times he saved Weeps from a mauling. But he didn't need to look after Wol.

There was a German shepherd who lived near us, and one day this dog met Wol out walking, and decided to see how horned owl tasted.

I heard the ruckus and came running. But by the time I got to the street Wol was sitting on the dog's back, digging his claws in for all he was worth, and ripping chunks out of the dog's ears with his beak.

The shepherd headed down Spadina Avenue *yip-yip-yipping* till you could have heard it in Timbuctoo.

Wol rode him for three blocks, and might have ridden him right out of town if the dog hadn't dodged through a hole in a board fence and knocked Wol off. I had chased after them on my bike, but by the time I got to the fence Wol had picked himself up, given himself a shake or two to settle his feathers, and was his usual friendly self. He gave me a cheerful "Hoo-HOO-hoohoo!" and jumped up on the handle bars for a ride home.

Word seemed to get around after that, and the neighborhood dogs took to crossing over to the other side of the road when they saw Wol coming.

Chapter 6

On the day school closed for the summer, the T. Eaton Department Store announced it was going to sponsor a pet parade two weeks later, and there were going to be prizes for the most interesting pets, and the best displays. Bruce was the first of our gang to hear about it, and he came right over to my house to tell Murray and me.

"Hey!" said Bruce, after he had told us all he knew. "With the animals we got, we could win a dozen prizes. What about it?"

Murray and I didn't need much convincing. We spent the next couple of days planning what we'd do.

First we decided to hitch Mutt and Rex to my old express wagon. We would fix it up with colored cardboard and stuff, so it looked like a circus wagon. We planned to put an old fur muff of my mother's around Mutt's neck to make him look like a lion, and we were going to paint black stripes on Rex so he would look like a zebra. Then we decided to build a circus cage on the wagon, and fill it with different kinds of gophers. Finally, we decided to have the owls riding on top of the cage, all dressed up in dolls' clothes.

We had two weeks to get things ready, and we really worked.

First, we built the circus cage, and when we were finished it looked just like the real ones that used to come to Saskatoon with the Bailey Brothers Circus every summer. Ours wasn't as strong, though, because the sides were only cardboard, painted red and blue and yellow. And instead of iron bars, we used chicken wire to keep the gophers from getting out.

When it was finished we made a hike out to the bluffs near the exhibition grounds, because that was a good place to find wood gophers. We caught six of them, and on the way home we snared about a dozen striped gophers that were living in a cutbank by the roadside. Together with the thirty ordinary gophers we already had, this added up to an awful lot of gophers, and there wasn't going to be room for all of them in one circus cage.

Murray fixed that.

"Why don't we make another cage out of my wagon?" he suggested. "Then we'd have twice as much chance to win first prize."

It was a dandy idea, so we went ahead and built the second cage. Then we decided to put some of our white rats with the extra gophers in the second one, to make it different.

The day before the parade—which was on a Saturday—we had everything ready. I had borrowed some doll clothes from Faith Honigan, who lived on the next block. Murray had got some washable sign paint from his Dad, so he could paint the black stripes on Rex. We had found a set of real dog harness for Mutt, and we had made a second set for Rex, out of twine. The cage-wagons were all finished and stored away in our garage so they wouldn't get wet if it rained.

On Sunday morning, I didn't even wait to eat my breakfast before I rushed out to the garage. Murray was already there, but Bruce didn't come along for about an hour, and we were getting worried he might not make it at all. By the time he showed up we had the gophers and the white rats all loaded and I was trying to get the dolls' clothes on the owls. Bruce came into the yard with a shoebox under his arm, and a big grin on his face.

"Hi-eee!" he shouted. "I guess we'll win the first prize sure. Bet you can't guess what I have in this box?"

Murray and I couldn't guess. I shook the box a couple of times, and whatever was inside was pretty heavy. I was just going to untie the string and open it when Bruce grabbed it away from me.

"No, sir," he said. "Don't you do that! We might never catch this critter again!"

"Aw, come on!" I begged him. "What you got in there, anyway? Come on, Brucie. You have to tell us."

"Don't have to—don't aim to!" Bruce said. "Just you wait and see."

Murray and I pretended we didn't care what he had in his shoebox anyway. I went back to putting the dolls' clothes on the owls, and it wasn't easy. Weeps just stood there and whimpered while I pulled a pink dress over his head and pinned a floppy hat on him. But Wol took one look at the sailor suit I had for him and then he rumpled himself up into a ball and began to clack his beak and hiss. It took two of us to hold him down while we got him dressed, and by the time we were finished he was in a terrible temper.

We couldn't trust him to stay quietly on the wagon-top after all that fuss, so we decided to tie him to it with some twine around his legs. That made him madder still.

While Bruce and I were working on the owls, Murray was trying to paint the stripes on Rex. Rex didn't like it, and there was about as much black paint on Murray as on the dog. Then Murray said he might as well finish what Rex had started, so he smeared black paint all over his own face and said he would go in the parade as a Zulu warrior.

Just before we were ready to start for downtown, Bruce took the paintbrush and printed some words on the shoebox; then he tied the box to the top of the second wagon. What he printed was:

SURPRIS PET Do NOT FEEED

We harnessed up the dogs, with Mutt leading because he knew how to pull in harness and Rex didn't. Rex didn't seem to want to learn, either. He kept pulling off to one side, and every time he did it he almost upset the wagons. We had an awful time getting our outfit all the way downtown and we were nearly late for the parade, which started at ten o'clock. One thing, though: by the time we did get there, old Rex was just about worn out and he had stopped acting like a bucking bronco.

The parade formed in front of the Carnegie Public Library and then it was supposed to go about six blocks to the T. Eaton Store, where the judges' stand was.

It seemed like a million kids were there with every kind of pet you ever saw. One little boy, about five years old, was leading a Clydesdale horse as big as an elephant, and the horse had BABY on the blanket it was wearing. If that thing was a baby, I hope to eat it!

There were a lot of goats, and it was a hot day, and you could smell goats all over Saskatoon. Some of the girls were wheeling cats along in baby carriages, and the cats were wearing silly hats and were pinned down under lacy covers. Some of them were yowling fit to scare the dead. There were more dogs than you could shake a stick at—every kind of dog you ever heard about, and a lot of kinds that nobody ever heard about.

Right in the middle of the parade was a boy leading a pet skunk on a string. He had the middle of the parade all to himself, too. Nobody was crowding *him!*

There were pet rabbits, ducks, chickens, geese, a couple of pigs, and a bunch of pedigree calves. There was even one little boy carrying a quart jar full of water, with a bunch of tadpoles swimming around in it.

You'd expect lots of trouble, what with all the animals and the fact that it was a hot day and everybody was excited and there was so much noise. But there really wasn't much trouble. There were dogfights, of course; and one dog, who wasn't even in the parade at all, made a go for a cat in a baby carriage and that stampeded one of the goats. But some salesmen from the store were in the parade too, and they got things quieted down, though one of them got bitten on the leg, a little bit.

It took about an hour for our outfit to get opposite the judges' stand. There were five judges, some women and some men. The Mayor of Saskatoon was one of them. There were two Mounties beside the stand, dressed in their red coats. A lot of parents were jammed up against the stand too, so they could cheer if their kids won a prize.

I'd had a good look at the parade by then, and there wasn't an outfit that had a patch on ours. We were sure to win a good prize, and I figured it would be first prize. We had a little trouble though when we got to the stand, because Rex was so tired he just lay down and wouldn't get up again. But that only made the judges laugh, and they came down from the stand to take a good look at our entry.

I overheard one of the woman judges tell another woman that ours was the best rig she had seen, and "Isn't it cute the way it's decked out just like a real circus?" The first prize seemed to be right in our pockets, when the president of the T. Eaton Store, who was also one of the judges, saw the shoebox on top of the second wagon.

"Hello," he said. "Now here's a good idea. Look at this, Sam! These boys have a special pet in reserve. That's what *I* call smart merchandising!"

Well, of course, everyone crowded around to see what the special pet was; and Bruce, with a silly smile on his dopey face, untied the box and lifted up the lid.

What was in the box was—a rattlesnake.

I guess you can imagine what happened next. All the people shoving and pushing to get away from us got the animals so upset that they began to stampede too. The skunk got crowded into a storefront, and that scared him, and he did what skunks always do when they get scared. There were calves and goats going every which way, and the dogs all went crazy and started chasing anything that ran—and that was everything there was. Our two cages got upset and squashed and all the gophers and white rats went skittering off under people's feet. Wol

climbed up on top of my head and kept beating his wings so I couldn't see too much of what was happening, but I could still hear it. Women were screaming, and one of the Mounties had hauled out his big revolver and was waving it in the air, while the other one never stopped blowing his silver whistle. All you could hear was yells and howls and barks and screams and yowls. I tell you, there never had been anything like it in Saskatoon for a hundred years.

We didn't stick around any longer than we could help. We saved the wagons, our two dogs, the owls, and that darn snake. Bruce grabbed the shoebox the moment the ruckus started and stuck to it like a bur until we got back to my place.

"Gee," he said, as we were getting a drink from our garden hose. "If I'd lost that old snake I'd have got my britches tanned from here to Mexico. It belongs to our hired man, and it's been his pet for fifteen years—ever since he was a cowboy down in the Cypress Hills. It's so old it hasn't any teeth, nor any poison either, but he sure is fond of it all the same. It sleeps right with him in his bunk. . . ."

I still think we should have won first prize.

Chapter 7

When the owls first came to live with us, Mutt didn't think much of them. He was jealous of all my pets, and he was particularly jealous of the owls because they took up so much of my time.

He never did get on very well with Wol, but after a few weeks he got so he could tolerate Weeps. I think this was because Weeps was so helpless, and because Mutt had to defend him from other dogs and from the neighborhood cats. And, of course, Weeps got very fond of Mutt, knowing he could depend on the old boy to protect him. Whenever Weeps was let out of his cage he would start searching around for Mutt. Once he spotted him, Weeps would give a little whoop of relief and go scuttling over to his protector's side. If Mutt was lying down, Weeps would snuggle in between his paws. Sometimes he would get so close that his "horn" feathers would tickle Mutt's nose, and then Mutt would sneeze and almost blow Weeps over backward.

If Weeps got to be too much of a nuisance, Mutt would try to hide from him, under the garage. But that wasn't much use. Weeps would squeeze under the garage too. He hated to let Mutt get out of his sight for even a minute.

Mutt's relations with Wol were another story. Wol wasn't afraid of anything that walked, flew or crawled; and that included Mutt. As far as Wol was concerned, old Mutt was something to be teased and pestered, and Wol used to tease the life half out of him.

Mutt was an absent-minded sort of dog. Instead of burying a bone he didn't happen to be using at the moment, he would often forget about it and leave it lying on the grass. That was a mistake, because sooner or later Wol would see it, swoop down and carry it off. It wasn't that Wol liked bones himself (not having any teeth, he couldn't chew them), he just liked to take them away from Mutt. Once he had the bone, he would put it somewhere where Mutt could see it or smell it—but couldn't reach it. Sometimes he would put the bone in the crotch of a tree just high enough so Mutt couldn't jump up and get it, or sometimes he would hide it in the gutters of the porch roof so that the nice rich bone smell would drift down and torment Mutt until he was nearly crazy.

Another of Wol's tricks was stealing Mutt's dinner. Mutt used to be fed on the back porch, about five o'clock each afternoon. When Wol was feeling particularly bored or ornery, he would play the dinner-stealing game. Having waited until Mutt started eating, Wol would scoot around to the front of the house and set up such a ruckus that it sounded like two dogfights and a catfight all happening at once. Mutt always fell for it. As soon as he heard the row he would come tearing around the corner, *woof-woof-woofing*, and ready for trouble. But while he was peering around in his shortsighted way, to see where the trouble was, Wol would have flown over the top of the house and be gobbling down Mutt's dinner on the back porch. When Mutt got back and found the plate empty he would look very puzzled. Being absent-minded, he couldn't always remember whether he had finished his dinner or not. All he knew was that he still felt hungry.

But Wol's favorite game with Mutt was the tail-squeeze.

Mutt was already a fairly old dog when the owls came to live with us, and during the heat of the summer afternoons he liked to have a snooze under the poplar trees in our front yard. He had hollowed out a bed for himself in the moist earth beneath the trees where he could lie in comfort until the sun started to go down and the air began to get a little cooler.

Wol, on the other hand, never seemed to sleep at all, although according to the bird books horned owls are supposed to sleep all day and hunt all night. Perhaps because Wol had never read those books he was just as active in the daytime as at night, and maybe more so.

On summer days, when I was away somewhere and there were no kids around to play with, Wol would get bored. That was usually when he would play the tail-squeeze game.

After first making sure Mutt was really fast asleep, Wol would begin to stalk the old dog the way a cat will stalk a bird. He always did it on foot; I think because he felt it wouldn't be playing fair to use his wings. Starting from the front porch, Wol would sneak across the lawn moving so slowly and carefully he hardly seemed to move at all.

If Mutt happened to raise his head he would see Wol standing stock-still on the grass and staring innocently up at the sky, as if he were wondering whether it was going to rain. After a long, suspicious look at Wol, Mutt's eyelids would begin to droop, his head would sag, and soon he would be fast asleep again. He snored, too, and as soon as the snores started, Wol would continue his slow and careful approach.

Sometimes it took Wol an hour or more to cross the lawn; but he did it so quietly and cautiously that Mutt never really had a chance.

When he had sneaked up close enough, Wol would raise one big foot and—very, very gently—lower it over the end of Mutt's long and bushy tail. Then Wol would let out a piercing scream and at the same moment he would give the tail a good hard squeeze.

Poor Mutt would leap straight into the air, yelping with surprise and pain. By the time he got his bearings and was ready to take a bite out of Wol, the owl would have flown to the limb of a nearby tree from which he would peer down at Mutt as much as to say: "Good heavens! What a terrible nightmare you must have been having!"

Mutt would roar and froth around the tree, daring Wol to come down and fight like a dog. Then Wol would make things even worse by closing his eyes and pretending to go sound asleep.

Although Wol loved practical jokes, the funny thing was that he never really harmed other animals if he could help it. Of course, if something tried to hurt *him*—that was different. Then Wol could be dangerous. But he certainly wasn't the fierce and bloodthirsty kind of bird that owls are supposed to be. He wouldn't even go hunting on his own; if a gopher or a white rat happened to get loose on the lawn, he wouldn't touch it. However, there was one kind of animal he would attack, and that was a skunk.

It seems that all horned owls just naturally hate skunks, though no one knows the reason why. What's more, horned owls are the only things I know of that will eat a skunk, and they even seem to like the taste.

Our house in Saskatoon stood close to the river, and along the bank of the river was a regular jungle of bushes and poplar trees which made an ideal place for skunks to live. Because they didn't have any enemies in town, the riverbank skunks had be-

come so cocky they would stroll along the sidewalk in front of our place as boldly as if they owned it.

That was before Wol came to live with us.

Cocky as ever, one of the riverbank skunks decided to take a walk down Crescent Avenue one summer evening just after Wol had learned to fly. The skunk came strutting along the sidewalk quite sure nothing in the world would dare to bother him. He ambled along, taking his own time, until he got under the overhanging branches of our poplar trees . . .

Mother and Dad and I were having dinner. The dining room windows were open because it had been such a hot day. All of a sudden there was a great *swooooosh* of wings—and there, on the window sill, sat Wol. Before any of us had time to move, he gave a leap and landed on the floor beside my chair. And he hadn't come empty-handed. Clutched in his talons was an enormous skunk. The skunk was dead, but that didn't help matters much because, before he died, he had managed to soak himself and Wol with his own special brand of perfume.

"Hoo-hoohoohoo-HOO!" Wol said proudly.

Which probably meant: "Mind if I join you? I've brought my supper with me."

Nobody stopped to answer. We three people were already stampeding through the door of the dining room, coughing and choking. Wol had to eat his dinner by himself.

It was two weeks before we could use the dining room again, and when Mother sent the rug and drapes to the cleaners, the man who owned the shop phoned her right back and wanted to know if she was trying to ruin him.

Wol didn't smell so sweet either, but he couldn't understand why he was so unpopular all of a sudden. His feelings must have been hurt by the way everybody kept trying to avoid him. After two or three days, when even I wouldn't go near him, or let him come near me, he became very unhappy. Then an idea must have come into his funny head. He must have decided we were mad at him because he hadn't shared his skunk with us! So one day he went down to the riverbank and caught a second skunk, and brought it home for us.

By this time he was so soaked in skunk oil that you could smell him a block away. Some of our neighbors complained about it, and so finally my father had to give Wol a bath in about a gallon of tomato juice. Tomato juice is the only thing that will wash away the smell of skunk.

Poor Wol! By the time Dad was through with him he looked like a rag mop that had been dipped in ketchup. But he got the idea, and he never again brought his skunks home to us.

Chapter 8

The banks of the Saskatchewan River were very steep where the river ran through the prairie to the south of Saskatoon; and about two miles downstream from the city was a perfect place for digging caves. Bruce and Murray and I had our summer headquarters down there, in an old cave some hobos had dug a long time ago. They had fixed it up with logs and pieces of wood so it wouldn't collapse. You have to be careful of caves, because if they don't have good strong logs to hold up the roof, the whole thing can fall down and kill you. This was a good cave we had, though; my Dad had even come there and looked it over to make sure it was safe for us.

It had a door made of a piece of tin-roofing, and there was a smokestack going up through the ceiling. Inside was a sort of bench where you could lie down, and we had two old butter-crates for chairs. We put dry hay down on the floor for a carpet, and under the hay there was a secret hole where we could hide anything that was specially valuable.

The river ran only a hop-skip-and-a-jump from the door of the cave. There was a big sand bar close by which made a backwater where the current was slow enough for swimming. Standing right beside the swimming hole was the biggest cottonwood tree in the whole of Saskatchewan. One of its branches stuck straight out over the water, and there were old marks on it where a rope had cut into the bark. An

Indian who was being chased by the Mounties, a long, long time ago, was supposed to have hanged himself on that branch so the Mounties wouldn't catch him alive.

We used to go to our cave a couple of times a week during the summer holidays, and usually we took the owls along. Wol had learned how to ride on the handle bars of my bicycle; but Weeps couldn't keep his balance there, so we built a kind of box for him and tied it to the carrier behind the seat. Mutt and Rex used to come too, chasing cows whenever they got a chance, or racing away across the prairie after jack rabbits.

We would bike out to the end of Third Avenue and then along an old Indian trail that ran along the top of the riverbank. When we got close to the cave we would hide our bikes in the willows and then climb down the bank and follow a secret path. There were some pretty tough kids in Saskatoon, and we didn't want them to find our cave if we could help it.

Wol loved those trips. All the way out he would bounce up and down on the handle bars, hooting to himself with excitement, or hooting out insults at any passing dog. When we came to the place where we hid the bikes, he would fly up into the poplars and follow us through the tops of the trees. He usually stayed pretty close, though; because, if he didn't, some crows would be sure to spot him and then they would call up all the other crows for miles around and try to mob him. When that happened he would come zooming down to the cave and bang on the door with his beak until we let him in. He wasn't afraid of the crows; it was just that he couldn't fight back when they tormented him. As for Weeps, he

usually stayed right in the cave, where he felt safe.

One summer afternoon, when we were at the cave, we decided to go for a swim. The three of us shucked off our clothes and raced for the sand bar, hollering at each other: "Last one in's a Dutchman!"

In half a minute we were in the water splashing around, and rolling in the slippery black mud along the edge of the sand bar. It was great stuff to fight with. Nice and soft and slithery, it packed into mushy mud-balls that made a wonderful splash when they hit something.

Whenever we went swimming, Wol would come

along and find a perch in the Hanging Tree where he could watch the fun. He would get out on the big limb that hung over the water and the more fuss and noise we made the more excited he became. He would walk back and forth along the limb, *hoo-hooing* and ruffling his feathers, and you could tell he felt he was missing out on the fun.

This particular day he couldn't stand it any longer, so he came down out of the tree and waddled right to the river's edge.

We were skylarking on the sand bar when I saw him, so I gave him a yell: "Hey Wol! C'mon there, Wol old owl! C'mon out here!"

Of course I thought he would fly across the strip of open water and light on the dry sand where we were playing. But I forgot Wol had never had any experience with water before, except in his drinking bowl at home.

He got his experience in a hurry. Instead of spreading his wings, he lifted up one foot very deliberately and started to walk across the water toward us.

It didn't take him long to find out he couldn't do it. There was an almighty splash and spray flew every which way. By the time we raced across and fished him out, he was half-drowned, and about the sickest-looking bird you ever saw. His feathers were plastered down until he looked as skinny as a plucked chicken. The slimy black mud hadn't improved his looks much either.

I carried him ashore, but he didn't thank me for it. His feelings were hurt worse than he was, and after he had shaken most of the water out of his feathers he went gallumphing off through the woods, toward home on foot (he was too wet to fly), without a backward glance.

Toward the middle of July Bruce and I got permission from our parents to spend a night in the cave. Murray couldn't come because his mother wouldn't let him. We took Wol and Weeps with us, and of course we had both dogs.

In the afternoon we went for a hike over the prairie looking for birds. Mutt, who was running ahead of us, flushed a prairie chicken off her nest. There were ten eggs in the nest and they were just hatching out.

We sat down beside the nest and watched. In an hour's time seven of the little chickens had hatched before our eyes. It was pretty exciting to see, and Wol seemed just as curious about it as we were. Then all of a sudden three of the newly hatched little birds slipped out of the nest and scuttled straight for Wol. Before he could move they were underneath him, crowding against his big feet, and *peep-peeping* happily. I guess they thought he was their mother, because they hadn't seen their real mother yet.

Wol was so surprised he didn't know what to do. He kept lifting up one foot and then the other to shake off the little ones. When the other four babies joined the first three, Wol began to get nervous. But finally he seemed to resign himself to being a mother, and he fluffed his feathers out and lowered himself very gently to the ground.

Bruce and I nearly died laughing. The sight of the baby prairie chickens popping their heads out through Wol's feathers, and that great big beak of his snapping anxiously in the air right over their heads, was the silliest thing I've ever seen. I guess Wol knew it was silly, too, but he couldn't figure how to get out of the mess he was in. He kept looking at me as if he were saying, "For Heaven's sake, DO something!"

I don't know how long he would have stayed there, but we began to worry that the real mother might not find her chicks, so I finally lifted him up and put him on my shoulder, and we went back to the cave for supper.

We'd had a good laugh at Wol, but he had the laugh on us before the day was done.

After we had eaten we decided to go down to the riverbank and wait for the sun to set. A pair of coyotes lived on the opposite bank of the river, and every evening just at sunset one of them would climb a little hill and sit there howling. It was a scary sound, but we liked it because it made us feel that this was the olden times, and the prairie belonged to us, to the buffaloes and the Indians, and to the prairie wolves.

Wol was sitting in the Hanging Tree, and Rex and Mutt had gone off somewhere on a hunting trip of their own. It was growing dusk when we heard a lot of crashing in the trees behind us. We turned around just as two big kids came into sight. They were two of the toughest kids in Saskatoon. If they hadn't come on us so suddenly, we would have been running before they ever saw us. But now it was too late to run—they would have caught us before we could go ten feet. The only thing we could do was sit where we were and hope they would leave us alone.

What a hope *that* was! They came right over and one of them reached down and grabbed Bruce and started to twist his arm behind his back.

"Listen, you little rats," he said, "we heard you got a cave someplace down here. You're too young to own a cave, so we're taking over. Show us where it is, or I'll twist your arm right off!"

The other big kid made a grab for me, but I slipped past him and was just starting to run when he stuck his foot out and tripped me. Then he sat on me.

"Say, Joe," he said to his pal, "I got an idea. Either these kids tell us where the cave is, or we tie 'em to Ole Hanging Tree and leave 'em there all night with the Injun's ghost."

Just then the coyote across the river gave a howl. All four of us jumped a little, what with the talk of ghosts—but Joe said: "That ain't nothing. Just a coyote howling. You going to tell us, kid? Or do we tie you to the tree?"

Bruce and I knew they were only trying to scare us, but we were scared all right. I was just opening

my mouth to tell them where the cave was when Wol took a hand in things.

He had been sitting on the big limb of the Hanging Tree and, since it was almost dark by then, he looked like a big white blob up there. I don't think he'd been paying much attention to what was happening on the ground below him, but when that coyote howled he must have thought it was some kind of a challenge. He opened his beak and gave the Owl Hunting Scream.

Did you ever hear a horned owl scream? Usually they do it at night to scare any mice or rabbits that happen to be hiding near into jumping or running. Then the owl swoops down and grabs them. If you've ever heard an owl scream you'll know it's just about the most scary sound in all the world.

When Wol cut loose it made even my skin creep, and I knew what it was; but the two big kids didn't know.

Their heads jerked up, and they saw the ghostly white shape that was Wol up there in the Hanging Tree. And then they were off and running. They went right through the poplar woods like a couple of charging buffaloes, and we could still hear them breaking bush when they were half a mile away. My guess is they ran all the way to Saskatoon.

When they were out of hearing Bruce stood up and began rubbing his arm. Then he looked at Wol.

"Boy!" he said. "You sure scared those two roughnecks silly! But did you have to scare *me* right out of my skin too?"

"Hoo-HOO-hoo-hoo-hoo-HOO!" Wol chuckled as he floated down out of the tree and lit upon my shoulder.

Chapter 9

Wol and Weeps were with us long enough to be well known in Saskatoon. Particularly Wol. As my father said, Wol never quite realized he was an owl. Most of the time he seemed to think he was people. At any rate, he liked being with people and he wanted to be with us so much that we finally had to stop trying to keep him out of the house. If we locked him out he would come and bang his big beak against the window panes so hard we were afraid the glass would break. Screens were no good either, because he would tear them open with one sweep of his big claws. So eventually he became a house owl. He was always very well mannered in the house, and he caused no trouble—except on one particular occasion.

One midsummer day we had a visit from the new minister of our church. He had just arrived in Saskatoon, so he didn't know about our owls. Mother took him into the living room, and he sat down on our sofa with a cup of tea balanced on his knee, and began to talk to Mother about me skipping Sunday School.

Wol had been off on an expedition down on the riverbank. When he got home he ambled across the lawn, jumped up to the ledge of one of the living room windows and peered in. Spotting the stranger he gave another leap and landed heavily on the minister's shoulder.

Mother had seen him coming and had tried to warn the minister, but she was too late. By the time she had her mouth open, Wol was already hunched down on the man's shoulder, peering around into his face, making friendly owl noises.

"Who-who?" he asked politely.

Instead of answering, the minister let out a startled yelp and sprang to his feet. The tea spilled all over the rug, and the teacup shot into the fireplace and smashed into a million pieces.

It was all so sudden that Wol lost his balance; and when he lost his balance his talons just naturally tightened up to help him steady himself. When Wol tightened his grip the minister gave a wild Indian yell, and made a dash for the door.

Wol had never been treated this way before. He didn't like it. Just as the minister reached the front porch, Wol spread his wings and took off. His wings were big, and they were strong too. One of them clipped the man a bang on the side of his head, making him yell even louder. But by then Wol was airborne. He flew up into his favorite poplar tree, and he was in such a huff at the way he had been treated that he wouldn't come down again till after supper.

Riding on people's shoulders was a favorite pastime with Wol. Usually he was so careful with his big claws that you couldn't even feel them. Sometimes when he was on your shoulder and feeling specially friendly, he would nibble your ear. His beak was sharp enough to have taken the ear right off your head at a single bite, but he would just catch the bottom of your ear in his beak and very gently

nibble it a little. It didn't hurt at all, though it used to make some people nervous. One of my father's friends was a man who worked for the railroad, and he had very big, red ears. Every time he came for a visit to our house he wore a cap—a cap with ear-flaps. He wore it even in summertime because, he said, with ears as big as his and an ear-nibbling owl around he just couldn't afford to take chances.

Wol was usually good-natured, but he *could* get mad. One morning Mother sent me to the store for some groceries. My bike had a flat tire so I had to walk, and Wol walked with me. We were only a little way from our house when we met the postman coming toward us. He had a big bundle of letters in his hand, and he was sorting them and not watching where he was going. Instead of stepping around Wol, he walked right into him.

Worse still, he didn't even look down to see what it was he had stumbled over. He just gave a kind of kick to get whatever it was out of his way.

Well, you could do a lot of things to Wol and get away with it—but kicking him was something different. Hissing like a giant teakettle, he spread his wings wide out and clomped the postman on the shins with them. A whack from one of his wings was like the kick of a mule. The postman dropped his handful of letters and went pelting down the street, yelling blue murder—with Wol right on his heels.

After I got hold of Wol and calmed him down, I apologized to the postman. But for a month after that he wouldn't come into our yard at all. He used to

stand at the gate and whistle until one of us came out to get the mail.

Our owls were so used to going nearly everywhere with me now that when school started that fall I had a hard time keeping them at home. I used to bicycle to school, which was about two miles away across the river. During the first week after school opened, I was late four times because of having to take the owls back home after they had followed me partway.

Finally Dad suggested that I lock them up in the big pen each morning just before I left. Wol and Weeps hadn't used that pen for a long time, and when I put them in they acted as if it was a jail. Wol was particularly furious, and he began to tear at the chicken wire with his beak and claws. I sneaked off fast. I was almost late anyway, and I knew if I was late once more I'd be kept in after school.

I was about halfway over the river bridge when a man on the footpath gave a shout and pointed to something behind my back. At the same time a car, coming toward me, jammed on its brakes and nearly skidded into the cement railings. Not knowing what was going on, I put on my brakes too, and I just had time to stop when there was a wild rush of air on the back of my neck, a deep "HOOO-HOOO-HOO!" in my ear, and Wol landed on my shoulder.

He was out of breath—but he was so pleased with himself that I didn't have the heart to take him home. Anyway, there wasn't time. So he rode the handle bars the rest of the way to school.

I skidded into the yard just as the two-minute

bell was ringing and all the other kids were going through the doors. I couldn't decide what on earth to do with Wol. Then I remembered that I had some twine in my pocket. I fished it out and used it to tie him by one leg to the handle bars.

The first class I had that morning was French. Well, between worrying about Wol and not having done my homework, I was soon in trouble with the teacher (whom we called Fifi behind her back). Fifi made me come up in front of the class so she could tell me how dumb I was. I was standing beside her desk, wishing the floor would open and swallow me up, when there was a whump-whump-whump at the window. I turned my head to look, and there sat Wol.

It hadn't taken him long to untie the twine.

I heard later that he had banged on the windows of two or three other classrooms before he found the right one. Having found the right room at last, he didn't waste any time. Unluckily Fifi had left one of our windows open. Wol ducked down, saw me, and flew right in.

He was probably aiming to land on my shoulder, but he missed and at the last second tried to land on Fifi's desk. It was a polished hardwood desk; he couldn't get a grip on it. His brakes just wouldn't hold; he skated straight across the desk scattering papers and books all over the floor. Fifi saw him coming and tried to get up out of her chair, but she wasn't fast enough. Wol skidded off the end of the desk and plumped right into her lap.

There were some ructions after that. I was sent to the principal's office and Fifi went home for the rest of the day.

The principal was a good fellow, though. He just read me a lecture, and warned me that if I didn't keep my owl away from the school in future, he would have to get the police to do something about it.

We finally figured out a way to keep the owls from following me to school. Each morning, just before I left, we would let Wol and Weeps into the kitchen. Mother would feed them the bacon rinds left over from breakfast, while I sneaked out the front door and rode away. It worked fine, but it was a little hard on Mother because the owls got so fond of the kitchen she usually couldn't get them out of it again. Once I heard her telling a friend that, until a woman had tried to bake a cake, with two horned owls looking over her shoulders, she hadn't really lived at all!

Chapter 10

Thirty miles south of Saskatoon was a little village called Dundurn. It consisted of a garage, a couple of houses, and two red wooden grain elevators. Between Dundurn and the Saskatchewan River was a huge expanse of virgin prairie, and right in the middle of it was a slough so big it was almost a real lake, even though the water wasn't very deep.

This lake was about the best place for ducks and geese and other water birds in the whole of Saskatchewan. The reed beds along its shores were full of yellow-headed blackbirds, bitterns, coots and grebes. Out on the open water you could sometimes see two or three hundred families of ducks—mallards, pintails, shovelers and lots of other kinds. Sometimes there were flocks of whistling swans; and in the autumn so many geese stopped to rest that they almost hid the water.

Every summer we used to camp for a couple of weeks near Dundurn in a four-wheeled caravan my father had built, which we used to tow behind our Model A Ford. The caravan was fixed up like a little ship. It had ship's bunks, a ship's galley (which is what sailors call a kitchen), ship's lamps, and a ship's clock. On deck (the roof), there was even a little mast with a flag flying from it. People in Saskatoon used to call it Mowat's Prairie Schooner. On a stormy night when the wind made the caravan rock back and forth you could lie snug in your bunk and find it hard to believe you weren't on a real schooner, after all.

Of course, whenever we took the caravan on a trip, Mutt and the owls had to come along. Our Ford was a convertible with a rumble-seat. (A rumble-seat, something cars don't have any more, was a sort of folding seat placed where the trunk is on a modern car.) This was where Mutt, the owls, my friends and I used to ride. Mutt always rode with his head and front feet stuck away out over the side of the car, while Bruce or I held onto his tail so he wouldn't fall out on his nose. The owls used to perch on the back of the rumble-seat, and they had to hang on for dear life.

Because his eyes used to get sore from the dust of the prairie roads, Mutt had to wear goggles—the same kind that motorcycle riders wear. The sight of a goggled dog, two horned owls, and our prairie schooner used to make people in other cars take a long look at us as they went by. Sometimes they didn't believe their eyes, and then they would turn their cars around and follow us to make sure they hadn't been seeing things.

During the second summer that the owls lived with us, we went to Dundurn for a camping trip. There was lots of water in the lake that year and my father brought along his canoe, tied to the deck of the caravan. He paddled Bruce and me all around the lake looking at birds. We must have found a hundred duck's-nests; and we even found the huge nest of a sandhill crane.

The first few times we went out in the canoe, Wol came down to the shore to see us off, but he wouldn't come canoeing with us. I think he still remembered the trouble he'd had with the Saskatchewan River, at the cave, and he didn't trust water any more. All the same, he hated to be left out of things. But when Weeps made up his mind to join us in the canoe one day, Wol got up his nerve and decided he'd come too.

It wasn't a very big canoe, and by the time two boys, one man, two owls and a dog had climbed in it was pretty crowded and pretty low in the water. We had to sit as still as mummies.

For a while Dad paddled in the open lake, and then we began to explore the reed beds. Soon we came to a muskrat's house with the nest of a mallard duck built on top of it. We had a look into the nest and were wondering how long it would be until the eggs hatched out, when a crow came swooping over the marsh.

He caught sight of our two owls, and just about went crazy. He cawed and cawed until, in about five minutes, the sky was black with crows. The more that came, the braver they all got, and soon they were diving down within a couple of feet of our heads. Dad tried to scare them away by waving his paddle and shouting; but by this time they were so excited they paid no attention to us. I guess no crows had ever caught a pair of owls at such a disadvantage before, and they were going to make the most of it.

Weeps scuttled under my seat and hid between my legs—but Wol, who was perched on the bow of the canoe, wasn't going to run away. He kept getting madder and madder until he was hissing and clacking his beak in a perfect fury. This made the crows even more excited, and some of them dived so close that the wind ruffled Wol's feathers.

Finally one crow came a bit too close. Suddenly

Wol spread his wings and jumped into the air; and at the same time he gave a sort of half-turn on his side and grabbed at the crow with both sets of talons. There was an explosion of black feathers and the crow went squawking off across the marsh, half-naked.

We didn't have time to watch him go. When Wol jumped, Bruce tried to catch him for fear he would fall in the water and be drowned. And that did it! Next second all of us, except Wol, were in the lake.

The water was only up to our knees, but the lake bottom was slimy black muck. As we scrambled to get hold of the canoe, Bruce and I and Dad got coated from head to foot with slime. Mutt, who had more sense than any of us, abandoned the canoe and headed for the muskrat house. Weeps, who must have thought this was the end, somehow managed to clutch hold of Mutt's tail, and was towed to the muskrat house. Wol, who had been flying when the canoe upset and who now couldn't find any place to land, kept circling over our heads, hooting at us to help him down. The crows were going wild; all the ducks and geese in the marsh were excited too; now they started to quack and honk until there was such a row you couldn't have heard a cannon being fired.

It took us nearly an hour to get back to shore. Dad pushed Bruce and me into the flooded canoe, somehow; then he waded ahead towing us. On the way we stopped at the muskrat house and rescued Mutt and Weeps. Wol finally grew so tired that he had to land somewhere, and he flopped down on my father's head.

This accident made us so angry with crows—any crows—that we could cheerfully have wrung the

neck of every crow in Saskatchewan. Next morning
Dad got out his shotgun and swore he was going to
even up the score. He decided he would hide at the
edge of a bluff near the lake, where the crows used to

gather, and try to call them into range of his gun with a wooden crow-call. Bruce and I and Wol went with him, but we stayed out of sight in the middle of the bluff while Dad tried to get the "black devils," as he called them, to come close enough to be shot.

But crows are wise birds in some ways. They can recognize a gun a long way off, and some of them must have spotted Dad's shotgun. He blew and blew on his crow-call, but though there were lots of them around, they all stayed a healthy distance away. Eventually Wol got bored and the first thing I knew he had walked right out into the open and climbed up on a fence post.

The crow-call hadn't worked. But Wol sure did.

As soon as they saw him the crows forgot all about being cautious, and about my father's gun; they gathered in clouds and began diving at Wol.

Dad couldn't miss. His shotgun was banging so steadily it began to sound as if a war had started. After each shot, the surviving crows would climb out of range. Then Wol would begin flapping his wings and hooting insults at them, and they would forget about the gun again.

The war with the crows lasted until Dad was out of ammunition. By then, there were a lot fewer crows around Dundurn.

When we got back to camp I was telling Mother about it, beginning with the way Wol had accidentally wandered out into the open.

"Wandered out?" my father interrupted. "Don't you believe it! Wol knew what he was doing."

And, come to think of it, Dad was probably right.

Chapter 11

The spring when Weeps and Wol became three years old was a very sad spring for me. My father had taken a new job, so we had to leave Saskatoon and go east to the big Ontario city of Toronto. There would be no more sloughs, no gophers, no bluffs and, worst of all, no prairies in Toronto.

I hated the idea of moving; but most of all I hated leaving my friends behind me—both my human and my animal friends. We couldn't take Weeps and Wol because they would have had to spend all their days locked up in a cage, and that would have been cruel. On the other hand, we couldn't just turn them loose either, because they had been members of a human family for so long they wouldn't have been able to look out for themselves.

All we could do was try to find someone who would give them a new home. I talked to most of my chums about this, and they all said they were willing to take my owls—but their parents wouldn't hear of it. Then, one day, I thought of Bruce. He and his family had moved away from Saskatoon a while earlier and were running a fox farm about two hundred miles to the northwest. I sat down and wrote Bruce a letter, and a few days later I got this reply:

DEERE BILLY:
    It is pretty good here. There are lots of ducks and we have started the fox farm and

got lots of pups. Dad says sure I can hav the owls. We hav a old fox pen I am fixing up to keep them and I am bilding a wood house in it to keep them warm. Rex is helthy and says hello to Mutt and says bring Mutt up here for a visit when you cum with the owls. There is a lot of Indians here and I go to school with a lot of real Indian kids. When you cum I will take you there and you can ride sum of their horses.

> So-long,
> Your old pal
> BRUCE

I showed the letter to my father.

"Sounds fine, Billy," he said. "What do you say we drive the owls up to Bruce's place on Friday af-

ternoon, and stay over for a visit until Sunday night?"

I said, yes, of course. And that was what we did.

It was a wonderful trip to Bruce's. The sloughs were full of water and the water was covered with ducks resting on their way north. We saw prairie chickens dancing on the side of the road; and there were more meadowlarks and red-tailed hawks than you could shake a stick at. The owls rode with me and Mutt in the rumble-seat, and they had a wonderful time. When we got to the farm, Bruce's mother had a big feed ready for us.

On Saturday Bruce took me to the Indian Reservation to meet his pals. One of them, a boy about my age named Harry Wild Hawk, loaned me a cayuse,

and the three of us rode all over the old prairie that day, chasing coyotes and jack rabbits, on horseback.

On Sunday Bruce and I stayed around the farm and I helped him finish off the cage where Wol and Weeps would sleep at night. That was a sad business, though, and I kept wishing that Saturday could have gone on forever.

Wol and Weeps didn't seem to suspect anything. I think they were having too much fun to be suspicious. Wol went off and explored the big poplar bluffs behind the fox farm. And then he walked all around among the fox cages, *hoot-hooting* at the foxes, and daring them to start something.

Weeps found his way to the meat house, where the fox food was ground up in a big mincing machine; and the hired man fed Weeps so many scraps that he could hardly walk at all.

Sunday night we put the two owls in their new cage. Weeps was asleep almost before I could turn the catch on the door, but all of a sudden Wol seemed to sense that something was wrong. He gave a funny sort of hoot and then he jumped over to the door and put his head against the wire mesh. I reached down and tickled him behind his "horns" for a minute and he seemed to think things were all right again. He climbed back up to his perch and fluffed out his feathers for the night.

I said: "Good-by, old owls. You look after each other. Someday, maybe, I'll be back. . . ."

A Note from the Author

Were Wol and Weeps real owls? Of course they were! And Mutt and Rex and Murray and Bruce and I were real. And if you should happen to be going to Saskatoon in the spring of the year, and if you should happen to take a walk across the prairie, it wouldn't surprise me in the least if you happened to meet some of us. And if it's a big white owl and a not-so-big brown owl you meet—give them my love, will you?

ABOUT THE AUTHOR

For nearly thirty years FARLEY MOWAT has written of the lands, seas and peoples of the Far North with a humor and raciness, an understanding and compassion that place him internationally among Canada's most distinguished authors.

Born in Belleville, Ontario in 1921, Mowat grew up in Belleville, Trenton, Windsor, Saskatoon, Toronto and Richmond Hill as his librarian father moved a household that included a miniature menagerie around the country; those early adventures were chronicled in *Owls in the Family* and *The Dog Who Wouldn't Be*. During World War II Mowat served in the army, entering as a private and emerging with the rank of captain. The experience of battle seared the imagination of the young soldier and ultimately gave rise to his most recent book, *And No Birds Sang*, a gripping eyewitness account of combat in Italy and Sicily.

Following his discharge, Mowat renewed his interest in the Canadian Arctic, an area he had first visited as a young man with an ornithologist uncle. Since 1949 he has lived in or visited almost every part of Canada and many other lands, including the distant regions of Siberia. He has said of himself, "I am a Northern Man ... I like to think I am a reincarnation of the Norse saga men and, like them, my chief concern is with the tales of men, and other animals, living under conditions of natural adversity." His experiences have inspired such works as *People of the Deer, The Desperate People, Never Cry Wolf, A Whale for the Killing* and *The Boat Who Wouldn't Float*. Farley Mowat's twenty-five books have been published in over twenty languages in more than forty countries.